The *Woman* I Met

KARISHMA SHAIK

First published by R&K Publications in 2026

ISBN: 978-81-999040-3-3

Cover design by Karishma Shaik

Published in India by
R&K Publications

Email: rkpublications.s@gmail.com

For anyone learning how to love again,
how to forgive,
how to begin.
May these words lead you
somewhere that feels like home.

CONTENTS

Chapter – 1

Chapter – 2

Chapter – 3

Chapter – 4

Chapter – 5

Chapter – 6

Chapter – 7

Chapter – 8

Epilogue

ACKNOWLEDGEMENTS

To my parents, thank you for being the quiet strength behind every step I take. Your sacrifices built the foundation I stand on, and your belief in me gave these words the courage to exist. Everything I write carries pieces of your resilience, your patience, and your love.

To my family, thank you for being my steady ground in a world that often feels uncertain. Your support has never been loud, but it has always been constant. You remind me who I am when I forget.

To my friends, thank you for listening to half-written poems, late night doubts, and dreams that felt too big to say out loud. You've turned my fears into laughter and my silence into conversations that shaped these pages more than you know.

To everyone who encouraged me to keep going when writing felt heavy, thank you for trusting my voice before I fully trusted it myself.

To R&K Publications, this dream began as a small idea and slowly grew into something real. This book stands as proof that faith and persistence can create their own path.

And to you, the reader, thank you for meeting her. If somewhere between these lines you found a reflection of yourself, a question you were afraid to ask, or a quiet understanding you didn't know you needed, then this book has reached exactly where it was meant to.

Chapter 1

1. The Woman We All Meet

They did not ask her
if she could survive what they chose.
They only counted years,
measured patience, and decided her body
was ready to be handed over.

Her parents called it marriage.
As if a word could excuse what was taken.
As if tradition could bleed for her
and still be holy.

They did not stop.
They did not look back.
They told her,
this was how women begin.

Still, she kept expecting kindness.
From strangers, mostly.
Because strangers had not studied
the exact places where she breaks.
Familiar hands knew too much.
They hurt with accuracy.

Sometimes she wondered
if anyone was meant to be gentle with a woman.
Not those who raised her.
Not the world that demanded her endurance.
Not even the child she carried,
who would grow up learning
what the world teaches everyone else.

I owe them my life, she knows.
But not the way *I was taught to live it*.
Not the shrinking.
Not the gratitude for pain.

This book begins here
with a woman who understands
that survival was never permission
to keep suffering.

2. *The Eldest Daughter*

Why does my worth live in your pride?
Can't I be loved simply for being me?

You call me your strength, your reason,
but sometimes I just want to be soft.
You see my calm face and steady hands,
not the trembling heart that hides behind them.

I have learned to smile when I'm breaking,
to carry the house in my small palms,
to stay composed while everyone leans on me.

Even pillars need rest,
even sunlight needs shade,
even the strong deserve to crumble once in a while.

You call me responsible, dependable,
and I am.
But some nights, I wish I could fall apart
without disappointing you.

The Woman I Met

I've learned to measure my value
in how proud you sound when you say my name,
but not once did you ask
how heavy that pride feels to hold.

I am not just your eldest daughter.
I am a person who still needs warmth,
not worship.

Even the ones who hold the family together
sometimes need to be held too.

Please, see me without the medals,
without the roles, without the perfection.

Love me in my pauses,
in my tiredness,
in the moments I am only human.

Because being the eldest
should not mean being the strongest.
Sometimes, I just want to be your child again.

3. At Her Expense

There are women everywhere,
holding the world together
in ways the world refuses to name.

Some wear uniforms and deadlines,
carry files, degrees, decisions.
Some stay within walls,
measuring days in meals, medicines,
school bags, and returning footsteps.
Their labour keeps lives breathing,
even when no salary arrives.

Some stand where society looks away.
Not because they chose ease,
but because hunger, history,
and men with unchecked power
cornered them there.
They take what should never be taken,
so that somewhere else
another woman sleeps without fear.

Do not mistake this for choice.
Do not dress it up as virtue.
This is what happens
when protection fails,
and women become the barrier
between violence and innocence
at the cost of their own bodies.

The world praises some women,
for being respectable, presentable, useful.
The rest are erased, blamed,
spoken about in lowered voices.

Yet all of them contribute.
Every one of them is paying something.

If you trace the safety of this world carefully,
you will find women underneath it.
Working, enduring, absorbing, sustaining.
Seen or unseen, named or unnamed,
the world keeps moving
on what women endure.

4. How Women Leave

Women have always known how to leave
without moving.
They vanish into daydreams,
into songs they hum while washing away the world.

They survive in half-finished journals,
in books tucked beneath pillows,
in the silence after everyone's fed,
where no one remembers to ask if they're tired.

They escape into stories
where love doesn't hurt
and choice isn't borrowed.
Where they can exist without apology,
and rest doesn't need permission.

Some run through memories,
some through future versions of themselves.
All of them learning how to disappear
just enough to stay.

Call it fantasy,
but sometimes the only way to endure
is to imagine softer worlds
than the ones they wake up in.

And still, they return,
not because the world softens,
but because they do.
They rebuild from fragments,
find peace in what remains,
and call it living.

Chapter 2

5. The Sky I Grew Up Under

The sky I grew up under
still feels like the same one.
Even though cities changed,
and I outgrew the streets I used to run through,
it still hangs above me like an old friend who never left.

I remember lying on rooftops,
counting stars I couldn't name,
believing every wish
was being written somewhere in light.
I thought growing up
would make the world bigger, not smaller.

Back then, the days felt endless,
and time moved with mercy.
Now I chase minutes the way
I once chased butterflies,
with too much urgency, not enough wonder.

Sometimes I catch myself
looking up the same way I did as a child,
half-expecting the clouds to recognize me,
half-hoping they do.

The sky has watched me change quietly,
through every heartbreak and new beginning,
through every version of myself
that learned to start again.

And maybe that's what growing up really is,
realizing nothing was ever truly gone,
just waiting above us, in the same sky
that never stopped believing we'd return.

6. The Girl I Used to Be

Sometimes I still see her,
the girl I used to be,
sitting by the window with a notebook,
dreaming of a life that felt too far away.

She believed everything could be fixed
with effort and kindness,
and maybe that was her most beautiful flaw.
She had no idea how much of herself
she'd give away trying to stay good.

There are days I miss her,
her certainty, her light,
the way she looked at the world
as if it was always about to love her back.

But growing up means learning
that even hope can bruise you,
and sometimes strength
looks like walking away quietly.

I wonder if she'd still recognize me now,
a little quieter, a little braver,
no longer chasing perfection
but peace.

And though I've outgrown her dreams,
I still thank her for believing,
because everything I am now
began with her faith
in what I could become.

7. *My Eyes*

My eyes have seen too much to stay innocent,
and yet, they still soften for sunsets.
They have watched love arrive like morning
and leave without closing the door.

They've memorized faces
that time refused to keep,
traced the outlines of joy
and the fine print of loss.

Some days they carry oceans,
some days, dust.
They have learned to hold both
without asking which one hurts less.

Through them, I've watched myself change—
the child who looked for wonder,
the girl who looked for love,
the woman who looks for peace.

My eyes are not windows anymore.
They are mirrors, reflecting the world
and everything it made me feel.

They have seen cruelty wrapped as care,
truth disguised as tenderness,
and still, they search for beauty,
even in the ruins.

If one day they close and never open,
I hope the last thing they see
is something kind,
something worth believing in.

8. The Child Who Still Lives in Me

There are moments when I feel grown,
steady, responsible, sure of myself.
I speak with confidence,
move through the world with intention,
and believe I have finally become
someone who knows how to stand tall.

But the spell breaks quickly
when a voice sharpens in the air.
All that confidence scatters like startled birds,
and the room begins to feel
too familiar for the wrong reasons.

I return to the little girl I once was,
the one who learned to shrink
so others would not feel threatened,
the one who swallowed her hurt
because no one ever asked why she was so quiet.

A raised voice does more than make my heart race.
It pulls me backward through time,
into memories I never chose,
into a childhood where survival meant staying small.

No matter how much I grow,
how much healing I gather,
she still lives inside me,
waiting for the world to be gentle just once,
to let her breathe without fear.

And maybe adulthood is not about erasing her
but learning to hold her hand,
when the world grows loud.
To tell her she is safe now,
even when her body forgets.

Breaking old fears is not a straight path.
But every time I choose to speak,
every time I refuse to shrink,
I become the adult she needed
and the child I am finally learning to love.

Chapter 3

9. When October Turned Into Us

They call it the month of turning pages,
where hearts either drift apart
or find their missing piece.

Under skies lined with lamps and fireworks,
I spoke the words my heart had been holding.
It was Diwali,
and somehow, the universe listened.

You smiled,
and the lights around us dimmed in comparison.
The air smelled of sweetness and spark,
but nothing felt brighter than that moment.

I didn't plan it.
October never asks for plans.
It just rewrites your story
when you least expect it.

Since that day,
even the ordinary feels new.
Every chat, every goodnight,
every small silence in between
carries that first confession's glow.

And maybe that's what the October theory really means.
Not losing or finding,
but realizing that sometimes
love chooses its own season to arrive.

10. You Were the Poem

You became a poem before I ever meant to write one.
Every thought of you found its way into rhythm,
every glance turned into a verse I didn't know I was creating.

You never needed grand gestures to leave your mark,
just the way you existed
was enough to fill the empty spaces in my pages.

Loving you feels like learning a language
only the heart understands,
where every moment becomes a stanza
and every silence feels complete.

When someone gives me a flower,
I think of you and offer them a garden.
Because love, when it's real,
doesn't return what it receives —
it becomes more with every giving.

So if someday

you find petals at your doorstep,

know this,

they bloomed from every memory

you ever gave me.

11. A Poet in Love

It used to be a beautiful daydream,
a place I'd visit when the world felt too real.
But now I catch myself touching my cheek,
just to see if I'm still awake,
or if you're only another vision
I've painted too perfectly.

You made me, a poet, forget my language.
Every word stumbles when it reaches your name.
And now that I'm living the dream I once imagined,
I don't know what more there is left to wish for,
because you've already blurred the line
between dreaming and being alive.

I used to write of love
like it was something distant and divine,
a flame I could describe but never hold.
But with you, even silence rhymes,
even stillness feels written.

Sometimes I fear I'll wake up,

and find that beauty this soft

was never meant to stay.

But then you smile,

and the entire sky seems to understand.

If this is what it means to love,

then let the poems go unwritten.

Because for once,

the story is no longer mine to tell,

it's something I am living.

12. Before Forever Begins

Why does love sound like a plea
and not a promise?
Why do we say “I need you”
instead of “I’ll stand beside you”?

Maybe we’ve mistaken attachment
for devotion,
the fear of losing
for the art of staying.

Maybe we’re too afraid
to smudge the first page,
too eager to keep it pretty
instead of honest.

Love was never meant to stay perfect.
It was meant to be lived,
to be messy, to bend, break,
and still choose again.

The truth is,
love isn’t about finding forever,
it’s about finding someone
who makes the present feel infinite.

They say even God once knelt
before love,
not in surrender,
but in awe,
because only love
can turn power into prayer.

Chapter 4

13. The Idea of Someone

Chronic single-d hits hard,
the kind that makes you laugh at your own loneliness
and still ache when love songs play.

The only guy I can think of
when I hear this song
is the one who never heard it with me.

It's strange
how I can write about love so well
and still not know how it feels in return.
How I can dream of hands I've never held,
and miss conversations
that never really happened.

Sometimes I wonder
if I'm in love with the idea of being loved,
or if I'm just building a person
out of all the things I deserve.

Maybe I'm not waiting for someone,
maybe I'm just waiting
to be understood
the way music understands me.

And until then,
I'll keep dedicating love songs
to the idea of someone,
the one who almost existed.

14. The Beauty of Impossible Things

Why do we fall in love
with what can never be ours?

Maybe it's because distance
makes devotion look divine.
Or maybe we mistake the ache
for something holy.

We fall for the almosts,
for the what-ifs that breathe
between reality and dream.
We convince ourselves
that unavailability is depth,
that longing is proof of love.

But maybe we love what we can't have
because it's safe that way.
It can't leave if it was never ours to begin with.
It can't hurt us the way real things do.

And yet, there’s beauty in the impossible,
in watching something you can’t touch
and calling it love anyway.

Because sometimes,
the heart doesn’t want forever —
it just wants to feel something
that takes its breath away,
even if it can never stay.

15. The Eyes I Once Dreamed Of

I have been in love once,
the kind that changes the way you breathe,
the kind that lingers even when you try
to forget its shape.
Some loves remain like old photographs,
faded yet impossible to throw away.

There are nights when I wonder
where life has carried him,
what doors he walks through now,
what mornings he wakes up to.
Our story became a memory,
but it still hums quietly inside me.

Somewhere in this world
a child will be born someday
with the same eyes I used to search for
in every room.
Eyes that once looked at me
like I was the entire horizon.

That child will never know
the oceans I cried for the one
who gave them those eyes.
They will grow up learning to smile,
to walk, to dream,
never knowing they carry
the face of my heartbreak.

Life continues for all of us
in ways we do not expect.
He will hold someone else's hands,
build someone else's home,
and the pieces of him I once loved
will belong to places I can never enter.

And still, somewhere inside me,
a softer truth survives.
Loving him taught me tenderness,
even in the ending,
and maybe that is the only part of him
I am meant to keep.

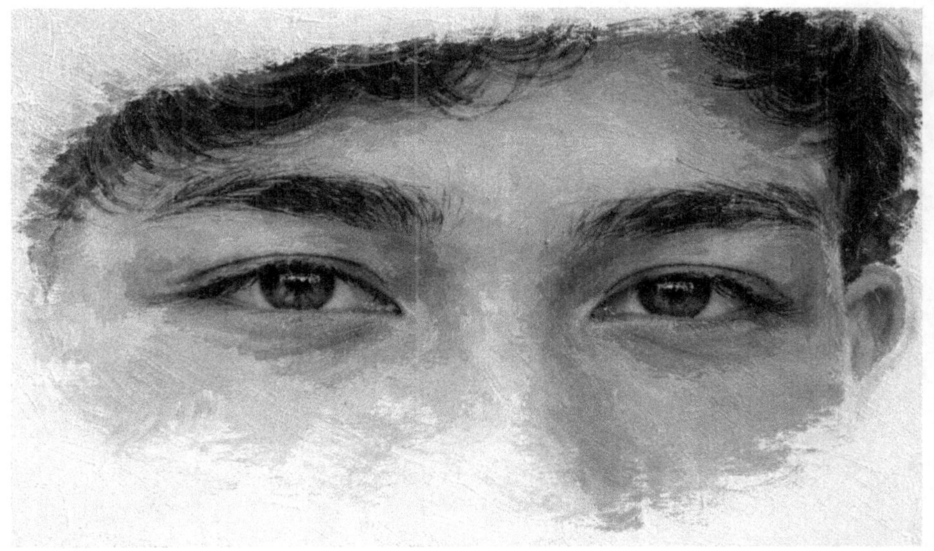

16. Even If It Burns

If someone can chase the smoke
knowing it will steal their breath,
then maybe it isn't foolish
to love someone who will never stay.

Some things aren't done for outcome,
but for feeling.
We chase what burns
because warmth feels better than nothing.

Maybe that's what love is,
a slow ache we choose,
a rebellion against reason.
We know it won't last,
but we reach for it anyway,
because how could we not?

To love is to risk,
to hold something fragile
and call it worth it.

And even if it ends in ash,
at least for a while, it felt like fire.

And maybe someday,
when the smoke clears and the ache softens,
we'll still call it beautiful,
the way it hurt, the way it burned,
the way it made us feel alive.

17. Repair Over Replacement

I wish people chose repair over replacement.
Everything would last longer —
not just things, but love,
and people too.

We live in a world
that gives up at the first crack,
that calls endings freedom
and patience a burden.
But love was never meant to be convenient.
It was meant to be cared for.

Once, people mended what mattered.
They stitched, glued, tried,
even when it wasn't easy.
They saw worth in what was worn.

Now we throw away what still works
just because it isn't shining.

We forget that even broken things
remember how to hold together
if given enough tenderness.

Maybe repair isn't about fixing what's damaged,
but choosing to stay
when it would be easier to leave.

Chapter 5

18. The House That Hurts

It's strange, isn't it —
how love can sound like comfort
and still feel like a cage.

They say family is everything,
and maybe that's why it hurts so much
to admit it isn't always kind.

There's warmth in their presence
and wounds in their words,
and I never know which one
I'll receive first.

The guilt of leaving
presses heavier than the pain of staying.
I tell myself they mean well,
even when their love leaves bruises
you can't see.

Sometimes I pack my dreams quietly
just to feel what freedom might sound like,
then unpack them before anyone notices.

Because how do you leave the ones
who taught you how to stay,
even when it breaks you?

I wish love didn't hurt like loyalty.
I wish home didn't feel
like something I have to survive.

19. The Flowers Died Too

The flowers died quietly,
like they were taught to.
No scream, just petals folding in on themselves,
a soft surrender to the soil.

I was bleeding through my eyes
and still got yelled for staining the blanket.
As if the proof of pain was more shameful
than the wound itself.

They rushed to wipe the mess,
but never asked where it came from.
It's strange how people fear the sight of hurt
more than the act of hurting.

The vase cracked days before,
but no one noticed.
They only mourned the flowers
when the water began to spill.

The sun still rose the next morning,
as if it hadn't watched everything wilt in silence.
Maybe even the light turns away from grief
it doesn't know how to hold.

The flowers and I,
we shared the same secret —
we both kept blooming for others,
long after our roots gave up.

I wonder if they'll remember me
the way they remembered the flowers,
for the way I looked alive even when I wasn't.

20. The Coffin

I built a coffin once, not for a body,
but for the versions of me that refused to rest.

The girl who kept saying sorry
just for taking up space.
The love that waited long after
the door had closed.
The hope that thought staying
was the same as being seen.

I lined it with letters I never sent,
with wilted petals that once knew what forever meant.
Candlelight flickered over the wood,
soft like forgiveness, and for the first time,
silence didn't hurt.

There was a name I couldn't say,
so I wrote it in dirt instead,
let the rain decide, what should stay.

Grief sat beside me, gentle this time,
her hands no longer cold.
She said, "This is not an ending,
this is compost, watch what grows from here."

And maybe that's what the coffin was for,
not death, but peace.
A home for the ache I carried too long,
a resting place, for the ghosts that made me human.

Because sometimes you must bury
what you swore you couldn't live without,
to give life, to the parts of you, that finally can.

21. The Garden You Planted

I hope you are here with me on this rainy day,
where my thoughts dig through my heart,
revoking that familiar ache you left behind.

The rain smells like the day you left.
I still remember the sound,
not of your goodbye,
but of the world becoming quieter
without you in it.

You used to say
rain makes everything new again,
but all it's ever done
is make your absence bloom louder.

The window still fogs the way it did
when we drew hearts that melted too soon.
The cup you loved sits by the sill,
half empty, half waiting.

I pass the garden you planted,
the one you said would outlive us.
The flowers still lean toward the light,
but none of them know who they're missing.

I talk to the rain now,
the way I once spoke to you.
It listens better than most people do.

And sometimes, when the thunder softens
and the wind smells like memory,
I almost believe you never really left,
you just became the weather I live beneath.

22. Too Gentle to Trust

I get nervous when beautiful things happen to me,
as if joy is a secret I am not supposed to hold.
As if the world will notice
and come to collect it back.

I have learned not to smile too wide,
not to breathe too easily,
because good things tend to leave when I do.

Maybe that is why I trace every moment twice,
why I keep memories folded like fragile letters,
afraid they might fade if I look too long.

Happiness feels temporary,
like the pause before thunder.
Even when life is kind,
I wait for the ache that follows.

I water my fears more than my dreams,
because they seem to grow faster,

and it feels safer to expect rain
than to pray for spring.

Some nights I think of all the times
I mistook peace for silence,
love for safety,
and wonder if joy has always been here,
just too gentle for me to trust.

Maybe this is how I survive,
by expecting the ending before it arrives,
so I can say I saw it coming,
even if I still break when it does.

Chapter 6

23. The Season of After

Even winter learns to leave
when it has nothing left to teach.
Even the moon disappears
to return whole again.

Grief doesn't leave all at once,
it lingers like rain
long after the storm has passed.
You learn to live with damp hands
and sunlight between the cracks.

You stop asking why,
and start whispering what now.
You collect the pieces,
not to fix what was broken,
but to build something new
from what survived.

Healing is the art of beginning
without waiting to feel ready.

It's watering the soil
where something once died
and finding green again.

So no,
we can't sit and stare at our wounds forever.
Some pain deserves to rest
in peace, not memory.

Even winter knows
it cannot stay forever.
So should we.

24. The Law of Exchange

Someone's happiness is someone's loss.
Even the genie, with all his magic,
never grants a wish for free.

Every joy hums with the memory of something gone,
every smile borrows light from an old ache.
The universe keeps its balance,
trading laughter for lessons,
beginnings for endings,
dreams for the courage to lose them.

Maybe that's why happiness feels fragile,
why love always carries a cost.
Nothing is ever given,
it's only moved,
from one heart to another,
from one story to the next.

I have learned to hold both—
the gift and the loss,

to thank the stars for what they gave,
even when they took something too.

And still, we keep asking,
keep wishing,
keep loving,
knowing every gift
comes with a shadow.

25. How I Count Now

I have seen people die,
and now I can't stop thinking of mine.

Their breath left like a candle
finally allowed to rest,
and the room learned how to hold its silence.

Since then, time feels borrowed,
days feel softer around the edges.
Every sunrise looks like mercy, every heartbeat,
a question I'm still learning to answer.

I used to plan years ahead.
Now I plan mornings, tea, sunlight,
the faces I want to remember.

Sometimes I look at old photographs
and realize how easily moments fade,
how memory is both a blessing
and a trick of the heart.

I think of the voices I no longer hear,
the laughter that ended mid-story.
And somehow, it teaches me
to listen better to the ones still here.

Death changed the way I count things—
not by gain or loss,
but by moments that still let me feel alive.

Maybe this is what living really means,
to hold life gently
because it could vanish mid-sentence.

26. The Last Seven Seconds

They say when the end comes,
the brain replays everything,
not in order, but in meaning.

In the first second,
you see a face that once called you home.
Not perfect, just familiar enough
to make you forget you're leaving.

In the second, you hear laughter,
yours, maybe theirs,
echoing somewhere the body can't follow.

By the third,
you're back beneath your childhood ceiling,
counting glow-in-the-dark stars
that never stopped shining.

The fourth is quieter.
You remember a smell,

the warmth of someone's hand,
how love once felt endless.
The fifth,
you realize it never really was.

The sixth,
you start to forgive yourself
for all the times you thought you ruined everything.
You didn't. You were just learning how to live.

And in the seventh,
everything folds together,
grief, joy, mornings, mistakes,
every person who ever touched your heart.
They all arrive at once,
and it feels like light.

It's not about dying.
It's about remembering,
the mind's last mercy,
to show you that you were here,
and you loved,
and that was enough.

27. The Way I Would Die

I am not afraid of death,
it feels like a quiet door closing
at the end of a long, gentle evening.

But I have seen death linger before,
its slow steps through the rooms of my family,
its cold patience taking one breath after another
until silence became the only thing left.

Those memories stay with me,
ghosts resting in the corners of my mind.
Sometimes I see their faces in the mirror,
and wonder if pain has already written my name.

Yet somewhere deep within,
I still wish to live fully,
to write stories that outlast the sorrow,
to see my family smile in the glow of what I've made,
to grow into the author I once dreamed of becoming.

If I could let go of the fear,
I think I would be the happiest person alive—
someone who wakes with sunlight on their skin
and gratitude instead of worry in their chest.
So I write, softly, patiently,
learning not to run from death,
but to remember how to live
like love never ends.

Chapter 7

28. Still Choosing to Sing

How can I wear the crown
when I'm still learning how not to bow?
How do I stand in the spotlight
when I'm still rehearsing forgiveness?

They say I was made to shine,
but I've been busy fixing the script
that told me I could only sparkle, if I never broke.

They call it grace, I call it survival.
The art of pretending you're fine
while quietly rewriting your fate.

I wear confidence like sequins,
each shimmer stitched over a scar.
They see performance, I feel prayer.

Maybe power isn't about being fearless,
but choosing to stand anyway.

To walk into the light
with all the shadows still clinging to you,
and let them see, you're still here.

I don't need destiny's permission anymore.
I'll tear the script,
write my name where it once said tragedy.
Because power isn't in the prophecy,
it's in surviving it.

29. *A Gallery of Goodbyes*

The woman I am today
was sculpted from silence and endings,
from every goodbye
I had the courage to walk away from.

She learned that closure doesn't always come
with kind words or soft exits,
sometimes it's just the sound
of your own footsteps leaving.

You can't stop people
from painting their version of you,
but you don't have to hang it in your gallery.
Not every portrait deserves your wall.

Let them create myths from misunderstandings.
You've lived enough truth to be art.
You've learned to frame your scars
as proof that you were brave enough to feel.

There was a time she tried to stay small,
to fit inside everyone's idea of gentle.
Now she's too vast for that,
too rooted in her own becoming
to apologize for her light.

The woman I am today
doesn't chase understanding anymore.
She simply walks away,
knowing not everyone deserves
a front-row seat to her becoming.

30. The Freedom I Have Not Lived Yet

They tell me I am free,
yet every choice I make feels supervised,
as if they trust my goodness but not my strength.
Their love becomes a constant caution,
a shadow reminding me what could go wrong.

They say the world is harsh
and I was born too soft for it,
but they do not see how much I want
to test the weight of my own courage.
How will I learn to stand
if I am always held by the shoulders.

They keep offering me petals
as if softness is the only thing
my footsteps deserve.
But I want the real path,
the one where the stones hurt a little,
where the thorns tell me I am finally alive.

I know they fear losing me,
But their fears cannot be my future,
I cannot inherit their hesitation
and call it protection.

One day I will walk the road alone
not because I wish to leave them behind
but because I finally trust
my own two feet.
And maybe then they will understand
that I was born to fly, not to be carried.

31. It Ends With Me

I grew up watching the women before me
carry storms as if they were seasons,
learning to survive instead of dream,
learning to stay silent instead of break open.
Their strength was shaped by endurance,
not by choice.

I saw their tears held back
so children would not worry,
their dreams folded away
so someone else could live freely.
Love for them was sacrifice,
never freedom.

With time I learned
that the world had told them
to shrink to fit inside a house,
to give until their hands trembled,
to forgive even when they were tired
of holding the pieces together.

But something in me refused
to inherit their pain and call it tradition.
I chose to listen to the voice
they never got to use,
the one that whispered there is more than this.

One day I stood tall enough
to gather the courage
they planted in me without knowing.
I said it ends with me,
not in anger but
in love for the women who raised me.

I am not breaking the chain
I am healing it.
Their wounds end in my strength,
their fears end in my voice,
and their dreams begin again
in the life I choose for myself.

32. What My Children Owe Me

I grew up believing
that children must repay their parents
with achievements, success,
and lives shaped by expectations.
It took me years to unlearn this
and see love with softer eyes.

My children will never owe me
a degree they do not want,
a marriage they are not ready for,
or a future carved by pressure.
Their life should not be a checklist
written by someone else.

What I want instead
is simpler than the world imagines.
I want them to breathe freely,
to feel safe in their own skin,
to know they are enough
without earning my approval.

If they laugh without fear,
if they choose kindness,
if they grow into people
who sleep peacefully at night,
then they have given me everything
I ever hoped for.

All I pray for is to be a place they can return to
without shame or hesitation.
If they grow up feeling loved
and happy in their choices
then that is all they ever owe me.

Chapter 8

33. The Color of Home

Brown things are beautiful,
like coffee, or someone's eyes
that make warmth feel like a promise.

Like the soil that holds beginnings
without asking for credit.
Like the earth after rain,
smelling of forgiveness and home.

Like old books with folded pages,
their words still loyal
to the ones who once held them.

Like skin kissed by sun and struggle,
soft, resilient,
a map of everything survived.

Like burnt sugar on fingertips,
bittersweet but real,
the taste of something that lingers.

Like the wooden floors of childhood homes,
carrying the echoes of laughter and loss,
yet standing strong beneath every step.

Like the shade of dusk
that wraps the day in peace,
reminding the light to rest.

They remind you of home,
of stories told in kitchens scented with coffee,
of hands that loved you without words.
And somehow, that's enough.

34. Dear Mom, I See It Now

I see it now—
how you always took the smaller plate,
the colder tea,
how you'd say you weren't hungry
just so I could have the last bite.

I see it in the way
your hands move faster than your words,
how care was always your language
long before I knew how to listen.

As a child, I thought love was loud,
something shouted from rooftops.
But yours was a whisper,
folded into every meal,
every sigh,
every morning that began with my name.

I never noticed
how much you gave quietly,

how much of your youth
was spent building my tomorrows.
I see it now, Mom,
in every tired smile,
in every scar that looks like sacrifice.

And maybe one day,
when I love someone like you loved me,
I'll finally understand
how love was never the words you said,
but everything you did
when no one was watching.

35. What I Have Now

What I have now feels almost sacred,
a home that hums with laughter,
parents whose voices still soften when they call my name,
brothers who bicker and still choose me first,
friends who remember my quiet days,
a love that feels like being understood.

Sometimes I pause mid-conversation
and think, this is it,
this is the part of life
I'll spend forever missing.

But having all this
has made me wary of the sky,
of fate and its quiet games.
Because now,
there's too much light to lose.

And yet, I keep my palms open,
because love was never meant to be held too tightly.

It asks us to stay,
knowing everything we touch
is already learning how to leave.

I've never been this loved before,
and I've never been this afraid
of losing it all.

36. The Moon and I

The moon and I understand each other.
We both show up every night,
pretending we're whole,
even when we're only half of ourselves.

I tell it things I can't say aloud,
and it listens without trying to fix me.
Its light never interrupts,
only lingers long enough for me to feel seen.

Some nights it hides behind clouds,
and I think, maybe it's tired too.
Maybe even the brightest things
need a little time away.

I've watched it change shapes
and still return again,
as if to remind me
that coming back different
is still coming back.

When the world feels far too loud,

I look up,

and there it is,

a familiar witness

to everything I never said.

Maybe that’s what comfort really means,

not being understood completely,

but being met halfway by something

that glows anyway.

37. What We Try to Hold

I have seen people lift their phones
not to record beauty but to record fear,
fear that a moment might slip away
before they learn how to live in it.
Pictures become proof that we were once happy.

We take photos of smiles that feel too rare,
of sunsets that leave too quickly,
of people whose presence, we are scared to depend on.
The camera becomes a shield against time we cannot control.

No one photographs something they are ready to release.
We only frame the moments, we want to stay longer,
hoping the picture will save, what memory might lose someday.
It is our small attempt at immortality.

Sometimes I look at old albums
and realize each picture was a fear in disguise.
A fear of losing that person, that place,
that younger version of myself
who did not know how fast life moves.

Perhaps that is why photos hurt and heal together.
They remind us of everything that once felt certain
and everything we had to let go before we were ready.
Pictures are the ghosts we choose to keep.

Yet I still take them
because love deserves witnesses.
Even if moments change, even if people drift,
I want proof that they were here,
that they mattered,
that my heart once lived in that light.

38. The Flowers We Save for Later

We always wait too long to say the words that matter.
There is a strange belief that people will stay forever,
that we have more time than the truth allows.

I have seen rooms fill with flowers
after a heartbeat stops,
as if beauty offered too late
could replace the warmth that is gone forever.
Regret blooms faster than gratitude ever does.

We hold back compliments
thinking we will say them someday.
We hesitate to call, forget to hug,
save our affection for a future that never arrives.

But the living need softness too.
They need to hear they are loved
before the silence becomes permanent,
before their chair is empty, before their absence
forces us to remember too late.

If only we offered the same tenderness
while hands were still warm,
while eyes could still soften,
while hearts could still answer.
Love should be a daily ritual,
not a delayed apology.

So give the flowers now.
Speak the gratitude now.
Do not wait for endings to make you brave.
Let the living feel cherished
before the world calls it memory.

39. The Anatomy of Feeling

I am made of the ache that makes me kind,
of the ocean that breaks
and still finds its way back to shore.

I am built from nostalgia,
the tender ghost that reminds me
how much I've lived.
From fear, the shadow that teaches me
how to hold the light tighter.

Guilt softens me
like rain on a sculptor's clay.
Love burns through me like wildfire,
and yet I keep walking toward it
again and again.

Choice is the trembling hand
that reaches for what hurts and still calls it hope.
Daydreams are the colors I use to paint over pain,
turning ache into art.

Because I am made of everything,

the fear, the love, the ruin, the rise.

40. The Weight of What Ifs

People leave differently.
Some slip away in silence,
as if their absence could go unnoticed.
Others leave in storms,
loud enough to make sure
you'll never forget the sound.

Some drift so slowly
you don't even realize they're gone
until one day,
their name feels foreign in your mouth,
like a language you used to know.

And still, we wonder.
What if they had stayed a little longer,
said what they meant instead of what was safe?
What if we had tried again,
before time taught us
that love isn't always enough?
Humans have this habit

of living in the ache between memory and maybe,
replaying moments
as if they might end differently
if we feel them hard enough.

But not everyone leaves in anger.
Some go because they've outgrown
the version of you they once loved,
and some because they finally found
the courage to choose themselves.

And sometimes, you're the one who leaves,
not because you stopped caring,
but because staying
started to sound like goodbye.

Now, I think love never really leaves.
It lingers softly in ordinary things,
a song, a scent, a season you can't name,
reminding you that what's gone
still lives somewhere quietly,
just not where it used to.

ABOUT THE AUTHOR

Karishma Shaik is a writer and poet drawn to the quiet places where memory lingers and ordinary moments learn how to stay. Her work explores love, womanhood, and becoming, shaped by observation, feeling, and the stories people leave behind. She is the author of *Where Footprints Turn to Stars* and *The Woman I Met*, and when she is not writing, she is usually lost in thought, noticing what others overlook, and finding poetry in the everyday.

Want to publish your own book?

Start your journey with R&K Publications.

R&K Publications is an independent publishing house dedicated to bringing authentic voices to life. We believe every story deserves a home, and every writer deserves to be heard.

To publish your book with us, scan the QR code below:

You can also reach out to us at:

Email: rkpublications.s@gmail.com
Instagram: @rk.publications

www.ingramcontent.com/pod-product-compliance
Lightning Source LLC
LaVergne TN
LVHW011047110826
845149LV00015B/3387
* 9 7 8 8 1 9 9 9 0 4 0 3 3 *